Hoodnapped (Robyn
Hood, Book 3)

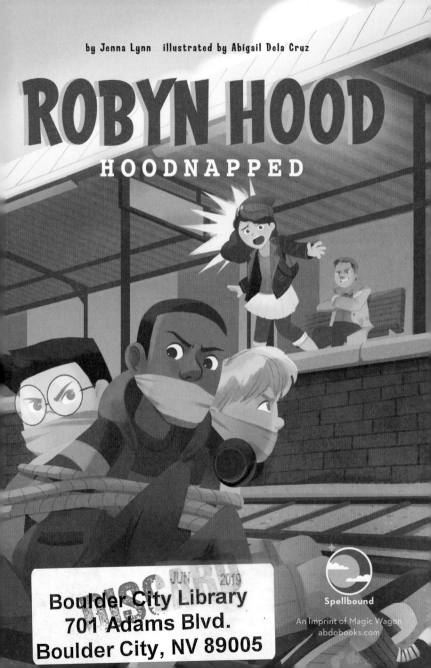

by Jenna Lynn   illustrated by Abigail Dela Cruz

ROBYN HOOD

HOODNAPPED

Spellbound

An Imprint of Magic Wagon
abdobooks.com

To my family, who have been my strongest supporters,
Dad, Mom, Zandra, Berna, Wowo, Mama and Tita Beth —ADC

For my family —JL

abdobooks.com

Printed in the United States of America, North Mankato, Minnesota.
092018
012019

 THIS BOOK CONTAINS
RECYCLED MATERIALS

Written by Jenna Lynn
Illustrated by Abigail Dela Cruz
Edited by Bridget O'Brien
Design Contributors: Victoria Bates, Candice Keimig and Laura Mitchell

Library of Congress Control Number: 2018947819

Publisher's Cataloging-in-Publication Data

Names: Lynn, Jenna, author. | Dela Cruz, Abigail, illustrator.
Title: Hoodnapped / by Jenna Lynn; illustrated by Abigail Dela Cruz.
Description: Minneapolis, Minnesota : Magic Wagon, 2019. | Series: Robyn Hood;
   book 3
Summary: The Hoods have been kidnapped and Robyn has to outsmart the villain in
   order to save her friends.
Identifiers: ISBN 9781532133787 (lib. bdg.) | ISBN 9781532134388 (ebook) | ISBN
   9781532134685 (Read-to-me ebook)
Subjects: LCSH: Kidnapping--Juvenile fiction. | Thieves--Juvenile fiction. |
   Friendship--Juvenile fiction. | Adventure stories--Juvenile fiction.
Classification: DDC [FIC]--dc23

TABLE OF CONTENTS

Chapter One

MISSING

Robyn Hood **sighed** in frustration as she checked her phone for the hundredth time. "Forty minutes *LATE!* This is bad even for them," she said to herself.

Robyn stood at the **outskirts** of Metropolis Market. She was **WAITING** for her friends Cole, Jasper, and Silas to arrive.

The trio, known as the Hoods, had a tendency to lose track of time while *GOOFING* off. But being this **LATE** for their daily patrol was testing Robyn's patience.

"Whatever, I'll do it myself," Robyn said as she **walked** into the **crowded** market.

Just a few **STEPS** forward and
she had already SPOTTED
her first pickpocket.

A man in a trench coat
LOOKED around
suspiciously. He was **REACHING**
for the wallet peeking out of an
elderly man's jacket pocket.

But when the man's **EYES** fell on Robyn, they widened in **PANIC**. He ran.

Robyn shook her head. She didn't have your average reputation for a **MASTER** thief.

Robyn preferred to use her skills to **HELP** people, not take from them. The other *THIEVES* of Metropolis knew they were no match for her.

Suddenly, she felt her **phone** go off.

"About time," she *mumbled* as she pulled out her phone. She expected a text from one of the Hoods. But the message from an **UNKNOWN** number stopped her in her tracks.

Chapter Two
FOLLOWED

Someone had **KIDNAPPED** the Hoods. A million thoughts raced through her mind, but they all came back to one. **SOMEONE** was using the Hoods to get to her.

"Stay calm, act like everything is fine," Robyn told herself. She **FORCED** her feet to move.

As she made her way toward the train station, she couldn't **SHAKE** the feeling that she was being **watched**. She was almost to the end of the market.

Out of the corner of her **EYE**,
she saw a **FLASH** of green.

Robyn *spun* around, certain
she'd catch the person who'd
been following her. She saw only
annoyed market-goers who
pushed past her.

"Stop being paranoid," Robyn *SCOLDED* herself. She checked her phone; only five minutes to noon. She had to *HURRY*.

Chapter Three

THE
CHIEF

The **TIME** turned noon as Robyn made her way to a waiting area bench. No sooner had she sat down when someone *slid* in next to her.

"Hello, Robyn Hood. Long time, no **see**."

Robyn was **SHOCKED** to find the voice belonged to the former Metropolis police chief.

He DISAPPEARED six months earlier after corruption charges were filed against him. Chief Alan was a wanted **CRIMINAL**. Everyone thought he'd left Metropolis for good.

WANTED
BY THE METROPOLIS POLICE

FORMER POLICE CHIEF ALAN DISAPPEARED WHEN CORRUPTION CHARGES WERE FILED AGAINST HIM. HE HAS TURNED TO CRIMINAL ACTIVITIES, INCLUDING ROBBERY. BEWARE. HE IS SMUG AND CRAFTY. IF YOU HAVE ANY INFORMATION ABOUT THIS CASE OR SEE ANYONE THAT LOOKS LIKE THIS MAN, REPORT TO THE METROPOLIS POLICE.

25

"What are you doing here?" Robyn asked in DISBELIEF. "Seems like I know a lot more about you than you know about me, Robyn Hood," he SNEERED.

"You see, I know that you fancy yourself a **HERO**. And I can relate. When I was police chief, I **LOVED** feeling like a hero."

"But you know what? Being a **CRIMINAL** feels even better. I take what I want, when I want, and I take out anyone in my way. And you, Robyn, are in my way."

"**Where** are the Hoods?" Robyn demanded. She didn't know if he was **STALLING** or just liked hearing his own voice. But she had had enough.

"That's the other thing I know about you, Robyn," Chief Alan replied. "You **CARE** about people, especially your friends. And that makes you **WEAK**."

Robyn grabbed the neck of his shirt and pulled him toward her. "**Where**. Are. The. Hoods." she growled.

The chief **laughed** as he pointed toward the high-speed train track. The Hoods were being **HELD**, bound, and gagged by the chief's henchmen.

Chapter Four

ARROWS

The color **drained** from Robyn's face. Her grip on the chief slackened. The electronic schedule board scrolled two minutes until the train arrived.

"Here's the thing," Chief Alan said. "I hate to **waste** talent. And I have to admit, you and your boys are talented. Now, everyone can **walk** away from this happy.

"All you have to do is work with me. For your first project, you'll **ROB** the riders on this train. Or you can **watch** your friends get run over. Up to you."

Robyn was **PANICKING**.
There had to be another way out
of this. But all she could think
about was the seconds **TICKING**
down on the countdown clock.

Fifty-nine, fifty-eight, fifty-seven,
fifty-six . . .

ZIP, ZIP!

"What the . . ." Robyn stared as two metallic arrows **FLEW** past her. They pinned the chief to the bench by the wrists of his jacket.

Suddenly, alarms **blared**.
Robyn looked up. Another arrow
had 𝕊𝕋ℝ𝕌ℂ𝕂 the fire alarm box
on the side of the station.

Security guards **RAN** out of the station to **see** what was going on. Robyn waved them over.

The guards immediately recognized the chief. They **CARRIED** him away kicking and screaming.

Robyn turned back to the track, **LOOKING** for the Hoods. They raced up and **EMBRACED** her in a fierce hug.

"How'd you guys get *AWAY*?" Robyn asked.

"As soon as those **GOONS** saw the guards, they booked it. Much easier to break free when your captors aren't **LOOKING**," Silas replied.

"Hey," Cole said intensely, pointing at a **SHADOW** by the station door. "I think there's someone watching us."

Robyn immediately *RAN* toward it. *Could it be the same person who was watching me in the market?*

But there was **NO ONE** to be found.

Robyn **LOOKED** over at the arrows now lying on the bench.

"Until next time, mystery follower."